Thank you for your support.

With Love,

Misty Blue Reign

By Mel Beng

Dedication

This book is dedicated to anyone who has ever doubted themselves for any reason. May you find the courage to believe in yourself and achieve your goals. Happy reading!

Mel Beng the Author

You can't go through something like that and come out the same.

-Misty Blue Reign

You don't stop reading a book because it has an ending. You keep reading to find out what's at the end.

-Mel Beng, Author

Acknowledgments

Thank you! I do not know how I could have completed this book without the love and encouragement of my support system. To my son Trey, thank you for always being by my side. To my Benguche family, my Mommy – Frances, siblings – Solomon, Colleen, Kavanni, Byron, Lascelle, and my niece Maya, thanks for the love. To my nephew Souljah, thanks for keeping me company. To my mom's handsome son Solomon Benguche who must have a special line because I won't hear the end of it – there you go – now leave me alone!

To Tameika Allen, thank you all the times I called cussing you out for pushing me past my comfort zone, Heyyy Girl! Thanks to my graphic designer Ashton Wagner who brought my cover to life. Thanks to Marlyn Vansen who is the model on the cover. Thanks to Bianca Scott with BusyB Writing for being the best hybrid publishing company. Your work ethic and commitment to excellence is what all self-publishing authors need through their journey.

To my Goal Friends Tribe, forever grateful! Tameika Allen, Kirsty Douglas, Shenika Ford, Fern Cayetano Adebakin, Kenisha Thompson, Felipa Benguche, Mary Lee Castillo, Marcie Neal White, and Andrea Steavison-Johnson, thanks to each and every one of you ladies for continuously pouring into me. I am so glad I have been able to surround myself with amazing women like you.

Special thanks to the members of my launch team: Glenda Curtis, Jade Smith, Katt Shaw, Dwight Elmore, Shelia Hawkins, Quintin Milton, and Tanjanik Munford. I appreciate you.

Lastly, I'd like to acknowledge me. You did it Melonie Benguche!

Prologue
Misty - Congratulations!? 1999

"Congratulations, it's a girl!"

Pink balloons fill the hospital room with various plush stuffed gray elephants. Lathan holds a baby wrapped in a pink receiving blanket covered with elephant print.

***

A knock at the door wakes Misty out of her sleep. The beeping noise from the machine running the IV began ringing loudly, alerting the nurse. Misty turned to look at the door and saw that it was her college friend Britney. She walks in and places her clear mini Tweety Bird book bag on the chair in the corner of the room. Seeing her friend's tear-stained face, she quickly grabs a washcloth, wets it with warm water, and scurries over to Misty's bedside.

"I'm so sorry Misty. I mean, you're young. You can always try to have another one after we finish college." Britney kept dabbing Misty's forehead with the cold, wet rag. The nurse entered the room and turned the beeping noise off.

"Do you need me to get you anything?" she asked while turning to face Misty.

"No, I'm fine," Misty exhales. She grabs her pillow closer as fresh tears roll down her cheeks.

"Girl, we can finish school. You can build TechNiche the way you have been talking my ear off about it. Hire me as your CFO. Remember, we got shit to do and millions to make," Britney continues to console Misty.

"Where's Lathan?" Misty asked.

"I don't know. I've been beeping him since I got here. He hasn't returned any of my pages."

"I thought this was a dream," Misty whispered, beginning to weep.

***

TEN MONTHS LATER

Cell phone ringing.

"Hello?" said Britney as she rubbed the sleep from her eyes.

"Code red, Bitch!" Misty yelled through the phone. "Come pick me up at the Motel 6 off of 76th Street. I just bleached this muthafucka's clothes!"

"Bitch what? Oh, my goodness. Are those sirens I hear? Bitch where he at? Bitch where you at? You know what, nevermind. I'm on my fucking way." Britney hangs up the phone and heads for the door.

Chapter 1
Reign - He put a Ring on it

Days turned into months of Reign and Brandon sitting in their respective corners of the four-bedroom house they shared together. Reign worked side by side with the interior decorator during the entire process. She wanted to be a part of every uniquely spectacular detail when it came to decorating the house. She hand-picked everything from the high-end luxury kitchen appliances to the T-shaped double barn doors of the master bedroom closet. The decor had a warm and cozy theme with blue abstract paintings on the walls that matched the candles on the coffee table.

Reign clutched her pillow while she sprawled out on the bed and gazed out the window. *I really outdid myself with this backyard,* she thought to herself. The backyard was created with perfection, with jubilant green grass and various colors of flowers that looked like something off the cover of *Better Homes and Garden.* She watched as graceful butterflies flew around the roses and bees danced from one flower to the next. While the summer sun was warm and shining brightly over the backyard, the beautifully designed master bedroom they shared was now a cold storage room for their clothes and jewels.

Reign reminisced about the days when Brandon was kind and considerate. He always made an effort to make sure she was okay and did thoughtful things that made her fall in love with him. She missed the little things he used to do, like open her door, send flowers to her office, and even send the random texts throughout the day. Now, she has her landscapers leave flowers on their deck to rekindle the feeling she once had during their honeymoon phase. Every week she switches out her flowers in the kitchen window that overlooked their inground pool to remind her of what used to be. These past few months, Brandon has become a complete stranger.

Reign and Brandon both had mastered the dance of avoidance. The most recent dance steps were now with one person walking into the room as the other one walked out of the room. The conversations between them reduced to going over the basics; "How was work?" "Did you eat?" "Did you pick up the dry cleaning?" "Did you get the milk?" Brandon's flights and time away from home increased, and their time together as a couple significantly decreased. As she tossed and turned on her bed, Reign tries to figure out when they transitioned from being a couple madly in love to now roommates. She turns and stares at Brandon's back as he gets up in silence for the third consecutive day.

"Good morning," greets Reign.

"Morning," Brandon mumbles. He picks up his phone and walks toward the master bathroom.

"What time will you be home tonight?" she inquires.

"Depends. Will I be coming home to an adult or an entitled brat whining about nothing?"

Reign sat quietly for a second. Her heartbreak didn't come from all Brandon's countless broken promises and disappointments, or from the fragrance of his cologne lingering in their sheets in his absence. It didn't come from the strokes of his dick when they first met, or the drastic reduction in orgasms she now experiences with him. It came from tying her heart to the perfect image of a life she created for both of them that she had on replay in her mind. When Brandon didn't play his part the way Reign had it scripted, her heart broke. What once was hours of passionate love-making, evolved to just busting a nut so they could be tolerable in each other's space, instead of discussing the love that had left the home they tried to build.

"Nice! Another day of you avoiding a conversation with your spats of insults. Look, your unexplained absences and unanswered phone calls are not going to be the way I continue staying in this relationship with you, Brandon, so I suggest you start making the necessary adjustments. Cause after today you won't have to worry about coming home to an adult or a brat, you'll start coming home to a bitch."

That struck a nerve. Brandon scowls and slams the bathroom door. A few minutes later, he walks out and grabs his wallet from the nightstand, throws cash on the bed, and slams the bedroom door without saying a word. Reign hears the front door slam, followed closely by the screeches of Brandon's tires as he pulls out of the driveway.

Reign knew her push for a conversation would trigger Brandon to disappear for a few days. She felt that she actually needed the break since she had to prepare for the few speaking engagements she had coming up. She did not want her current life issues and his negative energy to be the driving force behind her presentations. The sun sets and not one word from Brandon.

Merry Christmas

Reign sits on the faux fur sheepskin rug in front of the fireplace. She gazes at the lights on the Christmas tree holding a glass filled with Meiomi Pinot Noir, her wine of choice for the evening. The sounds of Mariah Carey's famous Christmas song, *All I want for Christmas is you* plays on Alexa in the background. She wipes away her tears of disappointment when her cell phone rings.

"Merry Christmas, Babe," cooed Brandon.

"Merry Christmas," Reign replies as she gets up and walks toward the kitchen.

"I'm sorry. I really tried to get back, but the weather is not on my side."

"I'm sure you tried. Took you a week to tell me that?" Reign takes a sip of her glass of wine.

"Well, this Christmas sucks," Brandon chuckles.

"It does. Guess we doing the remix. Seven whole fucking days, and not a word from you." She places her glass of red wine on the granite kitchen island.

"Babe, I really tried to get back. I'm sorry."

"Well, at least you're with your family. I'm stuck here by myself. I could have made plans to go see my family." She opens the refrigerator and grabs the last slice of red velvet cake she had been saving all week.

"I'm sorry. I don't know what else to say. I'm really sorry. Babe, I know we agreed to open gifts together, but I really want you to open one. Please don't fight me on this okay?"

"Hmmph. Ok, which one?" she asked as she places the cake on the island and walks back to the Christmas tree.

"I hid it in the back. It's wrapped in a light blue box with snowflakes. Let me know when you find it."

She pulls the gifts from under the tree and finds the neatly wrapped blue box Brandon described. After shoving the other presents back in their place, she puts her phone on speaker and places it on the rug. Upon further examination of the box, she started to get a little excited.

"I got it. Let me know when I can open it."

"Open it."

Reign rips the gift wrapping paper and opens the box. She gasps as she gazed down at the rock that was inside.

"I know we've been going through a lot, and now this Christmas has me stuck here away from you. I promise to make it up to you. I don't ever want to spend another Christmas without you, Babe."

"It's beautiful," she squeaks, holding the Cartier box.

"Will you be my wife?"

"Yes, Babe, of course, I will!" Reign screams as she places the 2 karat rose gold ring on her finger. Within seconds, she takes a picture and posts it on her social media sites. *I said YES!*

she typed quickly, not taking her eyes off her ring.

"Babe, I promise I will ask you properly when I get back, but I have to go. My family just walked in." The call ends abruptly.

Reign's phone rings, and she quickly answers.

"Hello?"

"Bitch, did that muthafucka give you a ring? What the fuck? Y'all just made up when, yesterday?!?!? And why you ain't call me before you started posting shit?" Storm yells through the phone.

Reign sits expressionless, staring at the ring. "I said yes?" Reign whispers in disbelief.

"Bitch, where's he at? Put Brandon's ass on the phone," Storm demands.

"He's not here. I thought that was him calling me back. I think his call dropped. Girl, you can yell at him when we get to Jamaica," Reign responds, changing the topic.

"Wait a damn minute. Bitch, just wait, hold up. Reign, did you put the ring on your finger yourself? Are you *serious* right now? I need to talk to Brandon's ass cause, Bitch, I'm so confused, and a bitch got questions. How you gonna propose from a whole nother fucking city?"

"Storm, calm yo ass down. We not getting married tomorrow, Bitch! Ugh! Have you finally decided on the damn color of this dress you got me wearing yet wit yo indecisive ass? You and Anderson keep fucking around with me, Imma show up on that beach at y'all wedding naked. Bouquet and all."

Reign was full of jokes to lighten the mood, but she knew Storm was right. This wasn't her ideal way to be proposed to, but at least it was happening...right?

New Year's Eve

Things were not necessarily perfect, but they were starting to look up for Reign. Her award-winning personal development workbooks were being sold in several bookstores, which were opening up more doors for speaking opportunities. She just bought a house, a new Jeep—in her favorite color blue of course—and now she is engaged to be married to her handsome fiancé Brandon DeVaugn.

Reign grabs her iPad and sends an email accepting her most recent speaking engagement with GraceStone Baptist Church in

Atlanta, GA. She was nervous yet excited because this would be the largest audience she would be speaking to as it relates to her workbook. After sealing the deal with her electronic signature, she advises the church's team of the forms of payments she accepts and when to pay her speaker fee. She notifies her team of the dates and requests that they start putting swag bags together for the guests she would be meeting after the service. Reign walks into the bedroom and puts the iPad on the charger by the bed. She checks her phone messages and returns it to the nightstand.

Reign hears Brandon in the shower and decides to join him. As soon as she opens the bathroom door, the shower stops.

"I wanted to join you," she says softly, handing him his robe as he steps out the shower.

"I've been in the shower for a while, but I'll wait for you." He takes the robe and ties a knot around his waist.

"No, go ahead. I'll meet you in bed."

Once she set the water temperature to her liking, Reign begins to undress and steps in the shower. On her way in, Brandon playfully spanks her on the ass. His smile has brought out a passionate intensity in her. It had been months since she felt love trying to creep back up between them. She was warming up to him again. She was more relaxed around him and felt adored when she looked back and caught him still staring at her.

The screeching sound of Brandon wiping down the mirror echoes across the marble tiles in the bathroom. She begins to lather her body with Olay Shea Butter Soap as the water runs through her tresses. When she finishes her shower, she steps out and wraps a towel around her hair, then puts on her robe. She looked up and saw Brandon still in front of the mirror. Affectionately, she wraps her arms around his waist from behind and buries her face into his back.

Unsure if it was the scent of two clean bodies or lack of sex between them, Brandon turns around and shares an intimate kiss with his fiancé. Lifting Reign by the legs, he throws her over his shoulder and carries her into the bedroom—hitting the light switch on the way to the bed. The only light in the room came from the television. He removes her robe, and with both his hands, gently cups her breasts, taking each one in his mouth suckling on her firm nipples. He spreads her legs and begins kissing her stomach, making his way down the rest of her torso. Intimately, he places her hands on his bald head, and Reign guides him to her already moist love tunnel. His tongue slides inside her, and he begins to unquenchably eat her like he was french kissing her mouth. Reign bites her bottom lip and gives into her weakness as she releases her warm juices into his mouth. He took his time, and she watches him lick his lips as he admires her neatly trimmed vagina.

Brandon pulls away from Reign and opens the top drawer of the nightstand to pull out one of her toys. He grabs her by the legs and continues to lick on her clit while gently sliding each anal bead inside her ass. Repeatedly, he traced the figure 8 on her clit, watching the cream trickle down her thigh. Reign squirmed as she contemplated grinding against his mouth or pushing his head away before he made her come. A low moan escaped her lips as he made her orgasm a second time. Reign tried to move, but Brandon held on tight, tongue-fucking her as the juices flow down the crack of her ass.

Pleased with himself, Brandon takes off his robe and lays on his back. His erect penis greets Reign, and she looks back at it menacingly. In one swift motion, she begins to gloss her lips with his pre-cum. She reaches between her legs and moistens his shaft with her dripping juices. With one hand, she mounts the base of his dick and, with the other, begins twisting his shaft. She starts to suck and used her firm tongue to make circular motions around the head of his penis.

"Mmmhhhmmm." His moans were music to her ears. She begins slurping and sucking the head in a soft, sensual, slow yet sloppy rhythmic motion. She released her hands from his shaft and took as much of his dick into her mouth as she could. Determined to activate her deepthroat game, she grabbed the sheets and clenched her fist.

"Goddamn, ahhhh shit, mmmm, ahhh, don't stop Missst," he whispers. Brandon grabs Reign by her hair, begins matching her rhythm, and savagely starts to fuck her throat. Her body was desiring him, making her want him inside of her even more. Reign could feel her warm molasses forming as it slowly drips down her inner thighs.

Reign picks up the towel, wipes her tears, and then the corners of her mouth. She blows her nose and throws the towel on the floor, ready to receive her man in the best way. She straddles Brandon as his dick finds its way inside her. He slides in her warmth, and she takes him all in.

The feeling of his dick and the anal beads is exhilarating. She watches her silhouette on the wall as her ass bounces up and down, riding his dick. The sound of the headboard hammering against the wall mixed with their moans kept her juices flowing down the shaft of his dick like a waterfall. She lowers her breast toward Brandon, and he starts to suck both of them at the same time.

Panting, she whispers, "I'm about to cum." He holds her waist and begins to rapidly thrust his dick inside her.

"Oh, oooh, ugh, ughhhh fuuuuuuck!" Brandon explodes inside of Reign and she collapses on his chest.

Chapter 2
Misty – Something Old, Something New

Misty sits quietly in her window seat and patiently waits for the passengers to exit the plane. She notices some people were rushing to get to their connecting flights, while others were moving at a leisurely pace to get home to their loved ones.

She turns her cell phone off airplane mode and watches as notifications flood her screen. While scrolling to see if she missed anything important, she sees the reminder of her 9:00 a.m. conference call with her team. Misty stands up, pulls her suitcase out of the overhead bin, and heads out towards the baggage claim area. She walks outside where the shuttle to the car rental awaits. After greeting the driver, she places her suitcase on the rack and finds a seat by the window as she sends a text.

It is June, why is your city so cold?

Misty flew into Chicago to meet Marcus Webb, the CEO of Webb Protect, which is one of the largest African American owned cybersecurity software companies in the city. This was her fifth trip, and while she loved visiting Chicago, Misty was becoming frustrated with the time and resources it was taking her to secure this new account with Webb Protect. She knows she has to be patient as it relates to this particular deal for her company, because working with Webb Protect would open the door for her company to expand into the Midwest region.

Five years ago, Misty risked leaving Corporate America to start her own IT consulting firm. She started with a laptop and a dream. During her humble beginnings of meeting in libraries, parks, and coffee shops, Misty took her time recruiting some of the best women of color to help build her business. TechNiche, now a multimillion-dollar company, has two offices—one located in Dunwoody and the other in Alpharetta, GA.

The all-women staff of TechNiche continues to break and dominate specialized areas in the IT world. It has won multiple awards and has been featured in some of the top magazines. *Wired, Computer World,* and *Digital Magazines* have all mentioned TechNiche as one of the top leading minority-owned and tech-driven consulting firms in the southeast region.

The driver announces, "Welcome to Enterprise," and opens the door to the shuttle. Misty walks to the front and picks up her suitcase. She tips the driver and walks through the automatic doors of the Enterprise building and stands in line. Suddenly, her phone vibrates.

```
I can warm you up 😉
```

Her phone vibrates again.

```
When were you going to tell me you were
in town?
```

```
                                I just did.
```

"NEXT!" yells a short Caucasian male from behind the Enterprise counter. He's wearing a yellow long-sleeve button-down shirt with a black bowtie. His eyes look exhausted, but his smile is warming. Misty steps up and returns the smile.

"Hi, do you have a reservation with us?" he asks.

She glanced at his name tag.

"Yes, I do, Ben."

She removes her driver's license and company credit card from her wallet and hands it over to him. While Ben types up her information, her phone vibrates.

```
I'm at work, I need my hug and my last
break is at 2.
```

Ok. I'll see you at 2.

It had been nine months since Misty last saw or spoke to Lathan. Their last encounter ended in a huge argument over an issue they had been arguing about for over twenty years. No matter how hard she tried, Lathan, for whatever reason, was the man she just couldn't seem to let go. Although they genuinely love and care for each other, they both realize they are from two completely different worlds. They simply couldn't do life together, but they also couldn't seem to do life apart from each other either. For some odd reason today, she is excited yet nervous to see him.

Misty signs the rental car documents, and Ben hands her the keys instructing her how to retrieve the vehicle. She walks out to the parking lot and presses the panic button on the key fob. A few feet away, the alarm of the black Acura goes off. She walks over and unlocks the door. After tossing her suitcase in the passenger seat, she climbs into the driver's seat and logs into the Hilton hotel app to check into her suite. She orders rooms service—a grilled salmon and steamed broccoli with a bottle of white Pinot Noir wine—then selects the time for delivery so that her food is warm and ready when she arrives.

She spends some time fumbling through the navigation system and tries to figure out how to connect her phone up to the Bluetooth. When the phone finally syncs, she hits the play button on her SoundCloud app and turns up the music to her favorite soca song, "Big Bad Soca" by Bunji Garlin. She learned of the artist on her first girl's trip to Trinidad and fell in love. She drives out the parking lot, admiring the red leather interior, and opens the sunroof to soak up the cool summer breeze of Chicago.

Misty's favorite part of Chicago is driving down Lake Shore Drive, especially at night. The city lights and the skyline captures a few of her favorite tourist sites—Soldier Field (the home of the Chicago Bears), the Field Museum, Buckingham Fountain, Millennial Park, and the Navy Pier just to name a few. The breathtaking view of Lake Michigan had a way of clearing and calming her thoughts. The Drake hotel was coming up, so she turns on the signal light to exit, and her phone vibrates again. *One unread message,* she thought to herself.

Misty drives to the door entrance of the hotel. With the increased visits to Chicago, The Drake has become her second home. Misty is greeted by a tall, handsome man, with shoulder-length dreadlocks and a captivating smile.

"Welcome to The Drake Hotel," he says as he opens the car door. His voice was deep and had a seductive tone that resonated in the words that left his succulent lips.

"Where's Manuel?" Misty asks.

"He retired about a week ago. My name is Eric. I will be handling your valet needs," he winks and extends his hand so Misty could exit the vehicle.

"I'll be sure to keep that in mind, Eric," Misty replies. She takes his hand and steps out of her Acura.

Misty climbs the stairs to the exquisite lobby entrance of the historic hotel. It is beautifully decorated with a massive orange Begonia floral arrangement in the center and huge chandeliers hanging from the ceiling. She checks in at the front desk to retrieve her room key and takes the elevator to her suite. When she gets to her room, she drops her purse on the dresser and walks over to the windows to open the curtains. She hears a knock on the door and peeps through the hole to see Eric looking back at her.

"I brought up your suitcase for you," he smiles, this time showing all his pearly white teeth and dimples.

"Thanks, Eric. I thought it was room service," she replies and steps aside to let him in.

"You can put it on the rack," she said as she held open the door.

"I'll check on that room service for you."

"Thanks, let me see if I have..."

"It can wait," he interrupts. "Let's get you fed first." He walks out and quietly closes the door behind him.

Misty looks at her watch. 11:45 p.m. She grabs her toiletry bag from her carryon and gets ready to go see Lathan. Standing under the showerhead, she lets the warm water run through her natural hair. She grabs the washcloth and begins to cleanse her smooth mocha skin.

Her body felt so good...she just had to keep caressing. Using her fingertips, she circles her clit, opens her slit, and begins to finger herself. The steam from the shower and the water running down her body turns her on even more. She squeezes her nipples, and after a few finger strokes, Misty starts to feel the tingling and tickling of a mini orgasm. Eventually, she gives in to her pleasure and releases her tension in the water. She washes herself up and turns the water off.

Misty wraps her natural hair in the towel. *I'll deal with these kinks tomorrow,* she thought to herself. She grabs the hotel robe from behind the bathroom door and walks out to the room. When she passes by the mirror, she stops for a second to take a look. Untying the robe, she starts to examine her imperfect curves of her body closely, with her hands on her waist. Her DDD breasts are perky with dark brown areolas, and her nipples stood firm from the cold air in the room. Misty looks at her vagina. *It's time for a wax,* she thought. Rummaging through her suitcase, she pulls out her Wonderlust perfume by Michael Kors. A little behind the ears, neck, and wrist is all it takes.

As soon as she finished rubbing the last bit on her wrists, there's a knock at the door. "Room service," calls a deep voice.

She ties her robe and looks through the peephole. *He better quit playing with me,* she thought as she opens the door.

"Grilled salmon, steamed broccoli, and your bottle of Pinot Noir wine. I brought two wine glasses just in case you have a guest coming," he says politely.

"This is my third time seeing you in one night, Eric. Valet, bell boy, well man, and now room service. Very impressive. Manuel leaves, and The Drake is falling apart," Misty jokes.

"I'm just making sure you're taken care of."

"Thank you." She pulls the cart into the room.

"Is there anything else you need?"

Misty unties her robe and puts her hand on her hip, exposing one of her breasts.

"I'll let you know if I need anything else, including you being my guest."

"Look forward to it," he smiles.

He walks out and Misty closes the door.

Chapter 3
Blue – Something Borrowed, This Damn Blue

My name is Blue, and this is MY story. Actually, Misty and Reign thought they could do a book without me and ummm… that wasn't going to happen! They have "images" to protect! That's them! I ain't got that kinda time! I may seem intrusive sometimes because I am. I also give advice that may come with my unsolicited opinions and unwelcome suggestions when I feel like it.

Let's get one thing very clear: when you have the urge to judge me, because I know you definitely will, please take a mental note, write it on a piece of paper, and share it with a friend. Listen. I. DON'T. GIVE. A. FUCK! Not about your opinion, your thoughts, or your perception of me. Before we move forward, I suggest you grab whatever you need to repent right now cause here we go...

I met Eric Hughes at The Drake Hotel in Chicago. I knew I should have left his ass alone when we first met, but my "big dick" radar went off when I saw him. He was the valet attendant, so I thought it was a nice gesture when he brought my food from room service to my suite.

When he walked in, my alert was confirmed when his cologne woke up my hoe-ly spirit. I immediately began mentally registering, *IMMA FUCK HIS ASS*. There was no second thought about it. I knew I was fucking him. It wasn't a matter of if, but *when*. I knew that before I checked out of that damn hotel, I was climbing his dick with no apology.

Ladies, I learned a long time ago there is a delicate line a woman has to balance between being a respectable lady in public and a freak behind closed doors. Recently through my life experiences, I've been saying fuck that line. Unapologetically owning your sexuality doesn't make you a slut or prude. There is power in the pussy. I strongly believe that a woman can only be free when she truly liberates herself sexually. While society ain't there yet, guess what? Society doesn't run my pussy. I do. I own my sexuality. I am led by my Hoe-ly spirit. That's been the best tool in my box. All women need to learn how to tap into the power and use it to their benefit. We all have that power. You better learn how to use it, Darling.

The night I decided to fuck Eric, I'd had a long ass fucking day, and Honey, a dildo just wouldn't do. This particular night I needed my back blown the fuck out. It was a requirement. I could not risk any batteries running fucking low that night, so I grabbed my cell phone and called down to valet. When I heard Eric's voice on the line, I said in the most Hoe-ductive tone I could muster, "At midnight, I need your dick and not my car." Didn't leave time for him to answer. I just hung up the phone.

I don't know if he's done this shit before, and he just may have. I don't even know if he knew who the fuck called. I simply made a request and hoped he came through. That's all I could do. Listen, I know I took a risk, but hey, life without risks is living no life at all, right?

Let's continue. Anyway, I am a big fan of self-care. I try my best to keep my nightly self-care routine, especially when I'm traveling because I have less distractions. I have a regime that meets all my five senses: seeing, smelling, hearing, tasting, and touching. If I don't know how to do anything else, I know how to take care of every sense of me.

See: That night after I showered, I had put my hair in two-strand twists. I slipped into my blue silk lingerie dress. I just love the way the color blue accents my mocha skin.

Smell: I had my lavender vanilla candle from Bath and Body Works lit. The aroma of the candle helps with my relaxation and fills the room with positive energy.

Hear: My homegirl India Arie accompanied me singing my song "Brown Skin" in the background on the television.

Taste: I sipped on a glass of Dolce della Rosa wine.

Touch: I apply shea butter lotion to my own mocha brown skin.

Like I said earlier, for my sense of *touch,* I needed a lil' something extra. I prepped Bishop as a backup, just in case. Remember, I didn't know if my request was going to be honored at this point of the night. Who is Bishop, you ask? Bish, that's my dildo's name. It's short for, Bish shut yo ass up! Honey, a dildo won't get you all the way right, but it'll sure knock the edge off. It can calm yo ass the fuck down, and you guessed it, Bish, it'll shut yo ass up—even if for a little while. So, Bishop just seem fitting. Back to what I was saying earlier, a bitch needed an extra touch to release. Thankfully that night, I didn't need to use Bishop, cause ya boy Eric came through for ya girl. Aye!

The buzz from the wine was kicking when I heard a knock on my room door. I looked at the clock. Bitch! It was midnight on the dot. *Punctual,* I thought to myself. *I like... Brownie point.* I walked over and looked through the peephole. When I opened the door, I saw him. I mean really *saw* him.

It must have been that lighting or something because I noticed things about him I didn't see when I first met his ass. Honey, there his fine ass stood at my door, six feet four inches tall. His dreads were pulled back, showing off his lineup as if he had just left the chair at the barbershop. The way the light shined on his scalp, you could see that he had recently got his dreads tightened. His thick eyebrows framed his brown eyes. They were a little puffy, probably from working overnight. His goatee was also neatly trimmed which helped highlight his succulent lips.

He had on a red V-neck t-shirt that showed off his muscular shoulders and gray Adidas sweatpants with red Adidas shoes. My thot ass eyes went straight for the prize. When I saw his imprint, my damn mouth watered. All I thought was, *Yo big dick ass betta know how to fuck.* I was so tempted to grab his ass cheek when he walked past me, but I behaved myself. Instead, I offered him a seat on the bed. He took off his shoes by the chair and sat on the side with his feet dangling by the headboard.

"Thanks for joining me," I flirted, as I handed him a glass of wine.

"Thanks for the invite," he responded, as he handed me a rose.

Push pause for a second.

Normally, even if you on a THOT move with yo hoe bag in hand, one would enjoy small chat to make it less awkward—even though y'all both know you both on some jump off shit. You talk about some random ass bullshit to make it less awkward, and it helps you justify in your mind you not really a hoe even though you doing hoe shit. You get me? Well, Bitch, this wasn't that type of night for me. This was *not* the night for fellowship. I was horny as fuck, and I had to go to work in the morning. I went straight to it.

Press play, let's continue.

"Take your clothes off," I demanded. He immediately obliged. Eric pulled off his shirt and dropped his sweatpants to the floor. He stood in his socks by the bed.

"Did you come up here ashy with no draws on?!" I laughed.

"I just took a shower," he shrugged.

"Lay yo ashy ass down so I can lotion that ass I've been wanting to touch."

"Where yo draws at?" he asked.

"It's in the bag. You want me to put them on?" I looked at him.

"Nah," he quickly responded and laid on his back.

"Turn around, I want to rub your ass, not your dick!"

I squeezed the lotion I was using in my hand and climbed on his lower back. I rubbed my hands together to warm the lotion and started to massage his shoulders. The heat from his body started to arouse me to the point I found myself dripping.

"I think you're enjoying this massage more than me," he said.

I chuckled. "Maybe. So what?"

He got up and asked me to lay down on my back. "Do you mind if I taste you?" Eric asked.

"Not at all," I whispered. He spread my legs and pulled my hips closer to him, putting my legs on his shoulders. He began kissing my inner thighs. Then he used his tongue to trace the outer layer of my pussy lips and gently make circular motions around my clit. He slid his middle finger inside of me and began to finger fuck me while he sucked my clit. A moan escaped my mouth. I took his middle finger and sucked off my juices to shut myself up. He began to stroke me with his firm tongue, causing my body to produce the natural nectar he was looking for. I held his head with both my hands and grinded my hips as I melted in his mouth.

When Eric finally released me, Baby, my legs were limp as fuck. He got on his knees, and his muthafucking dick stood at attention. Just *ready*. It hung nicely with a curve. I stretched over to the nightstand and grabbed a condom. The clock read 1:33 a.m. *Fuck work,* I thought to myself. It'll be okay.

Chapter 4
Reign – He said "I do" and it wasn't you!

The cell phone rings, waking up Reign. Brandon was no longer in bed. She looked at the phone screen reading PRIVATE. And presses the red button as she readjusts her pillow. The phone rings again. PRIVATE.

"Hello?" she answers with a groggy voice.

"Is this Reign?" an unknown woman questions.

Reign clears her throat and sits up in the bed. "It is 3 o'clock in the morning. Who is this?"

"This is Mrs. Christine DeVaughn," the woman continues. "You need to stop fucking my husband."

"Excuse me! What the fuck? Christine? You said Christine, right? I have no idea who or what you are talking about."

"I suggest you do your fucking research before making engagement announcements on social media with someone else's husband. Mr. Allen Brandon DeVaughn is *my* husband, and we share two children. I'm warning you now, hoe, STAY THE FUCK AWAY FROM MY GODDAMN HUSBAND! YOU HOMEWRECKING BITCH!" Christine snaps before hanging up.

Reign got up from the bed and looked around the room. Empty! Brandon's side of the bed. Empty! His closet. Empty! She turns on the security cameras and watches Brandon and two men load his stuff into his truck. She walks over to the fireplace and watches the few pictures they shared, burning! Reign bends over, holding her knees heavily, breathing in and out to catch her breath. The bellow of her cry sends tremors through her body as she falls to the ground.

Her phone vibrates. She sat on the bed, emotionlessly looking at the picture. It is her fiancé Brandon, his wife Christine, and their two children. A little boy who looked around five and a little girl looking just like him, probably about two years old. In the background sat Brandon's black F150 Ford truck. She knew it was recent because it showed the custom black lined rims she bought him two months ago for his birthday.

Reign throws her phone across the room and begins to cry uncontrollably. This call would be the first fall of a domino effect that would start the full speed downward spiral of the life Reign took years to build.

April Showers

It was the annual Women's Day celebration at GraceStone Baptist Church in Atlanta, GA. The day was finally here. With a congregation of close to an estimated thousand people, this would be Reign's largest audience in her speaking career. She never thought her gift would grow to this magnitude.

This would be Reign's first appearance after Brandon walked out of her life. These past few weeks were rough for her team. They were under major damage control due to Reign's unpredictable behavior. She was either canceling appearances at the last minute or was a no-show for scheduled speaking engagements.

Reign found herself at a crossroads with her relationship with God. She was painfully coming to terms with the fact that her world has crumbled. She wanted to go into GraceStone and have her message encourage the women in the congregation, but she was afraid that her personal struggles, resentment, anger, and disappointment would take over.

Reign sits with her head resting on her arms, holding onto the steering wheel of the SUV. She had instrumental gospel music playing in the background to mentally prepare for the morning message. Closing her eyes, she started thinking of ways to convince herself that she was ok. *Reign, you can do it,* she thought to herself. She is startled by a tap on her window and looks to see what caused it. There stood an older woman with red spectacles covering her round face. She wore a huge black church hat with a red feather on the side, and a silver rhinestone flower hung on her red blazer. Her eyes burned with motherly concern as she peered into the car. Curious, Reign rolled down her window.

"My name is Mother Blazemore," the woman said gently. "Honey, you ok?"

"Yes ma'am. Just praying," Reign replies, as a tear rolls down her cheek.

"Don't cry, Sweetie. Whatever you're going through, give it over to God. He'll take care of it for you. He'll never give you anything more than you can bear." She pats Reign on the shoulder and heads toward the side door of the church.

Reign grabs a couple of tissues from her console and dries her tears. She checks her watch to see how much time she had. 10:23 a.m. *Show time*, she thought as she rummaged through her bag for her lipstick. *One more coat won't hurt anything.* She checks her iPad battery and puts it in her purse along with a couple of her signed workbooks. After one last glance in the mirror, she heads into the church.

Reign is briefed by the service coordinator and confirms her notes for the audio and visual team. She is escorted into the sanctuary by two men from GraceStone's usher ministry. They walk into a large contemporary design sanctuary with purple chairs filled with churchgoers. The stage is covered in hardwood flooring, stuck between two large screens showing visual props for the congregation. A huge wooden cross hung above the audience to enhance the worship experience.

Reign is seated in the front row next to one of the elders. According to the program, after the choir finished singing, she would be next to speak. She listens as the band transitions to the next song and starts to play an instrumental introduction. The pianist majestically enhances the worship experience, playing the keyboard as if God was the only one in the entire sanctuary. Within a few notes, the song resonates, and Reign experiences a sense of peace. The lead singer steps out of the choir and walks over to the microphone. Her black glitter heels sparkle from the overhead lights on the stage. She is dressed in a fitted red pants suit, with a short bob haircut that frames her oval face. She looks directly into Reign's eyes and begins to sing.

Reign's eyes start to tear up. She stands up as the lyrics to the song, "It ain't ova" by Maurette Clark Brown continues to speak life into her spirit. She allows the tears to flow down her cheeks to cleanse her heart of the burdens she's been carrying.

When the song finishes, the lead singer and the choir exit the stage. Reign regains her composure and wipes her tears. She climbs the stairs and places her iPad on the podium. She grabs the microphone from the stand, and in a loud voice to the congregation, Reign begins to speak.

"The song says...BUT *THE IMPOSSIBLE IS GOD'S CHANCE TO WORK A MIRACLE. SO JUST KNOW, IT AIN'T OVA!* Oh, it's me, it's me, it's me, Oh, Lord, and I'm the one who is standing in need of prayer." The congregation stood up and began to clap, cheer, yell, scream, and cry out.

Reign continues, "Did anybody come to be transformed? Did anybody come to be pushed into the next realm of their dimension? Did anybody come because they needed to hear from God? Did anybody come because their destiny is on the line? If that's you, GraceStone, let me hear the sound of expectation." The congregation continues to clap and cheer even louder.

Reign walks back and places the microphone on the stand of the podium. She does a quick glance through the congregation and recognizes a familiar face. *I know this muthafucking Brandon did not bring his wife!*

Quickly, she darts her attention to her iPad, hoping that the camera whose televised broadcasts are beamed across the nation didn't capture her reaction.

Chapter 5
Flash Flood Warning

Misty adjusts her boobs for cleavage in her black lace bra and runs her fingers across her matching thong panties. She puts on her baby blue Nike jogging suit and sprays perfume behind her ears. Walking over to the living room area of the suite, she sits to tie her white on white Nike shoes then checks her watch. 1:45 a.m. *Ugh, I'm glad he's around the corner,* she thought to herself. She calls down to valet to prepare her vehicle, secretly hoping it would be Eric. Instead, a man with an accent answers the phone. She grabs her purse and heads to the elevator.

The valet attendant brought the Acura to the front door. Misty tips him and gets in her car. As soon as she turns the corner to go to

Northwestern Hospital, she presses the phone on the navigation system. "Call Lathan," she said clearly.

The phone dials, and a deep voice greets her. "Hello?"

"I'm outside," says Misty.

"Aight here I come," Lathan responds and ends the call.

Lathan walks outside the building. *Damn! He's fine as fuck even in his uniform,* she thinks to herself. He opens her door, allows Misty to step out of the Acura, and leans on the closed door. She wraps her arms around his broad shoulders, kissing his lips gently to greet him. He intensely returns her kiss, making sure to grab a handful of her ass in the process. Not too eager to let him go, she puts her head on his chest and wraps her arms around his waist. The scent of his cologne makes her melt.

"It's 2 in the morning. Where you going all dressed up?" Lathan asks. "I'm in this bum ass uniform."

"Meeting this handsome dude in his bum ass uniform to give him the hug he asked for. How have you been?" Misty teases.

"I'm good. Happy to see you. You know I'm always happy to see you."

He pulls Misty in closer and rests his chin on her forehead. *Safety*. After a few minutes of listening to the early morning quiet and holding each other, she whispers, "I miss you too."

"Damn, Babe," he said kissing her forehead, "You gotta stop popping in on me like this. You know I work these bullshit ass hours. How long you gone be here? Where you staying? Can I at least feed you?"

"I know. I'm here for the week. Staying at The Drake around the corner."

"Okay, I'm off on Tuesday, so we'll have to catch up then. But I gotta get back inside, Babe. You know my team can't do shit without me standing there."

"Ugh, I know." Reluctantly, she lets him go.

"Aight, Babe, I'll see you Tuesday. And don't hang up on me again, Punk. I'll call you when I get up." He opens the door, and she gets in the car. He holds her face in his hands, then kisses her forehead, her nose, and her lips.

"Ok."

"That's my Giblet."

"You keep me wet!" she laughs.

Lathan leans in and kisses her on the lips one last time before closing the door. She watches Lathan as he enters the building. She pulls out her phone and replies to the unread message.

OMW to flood your face. Thirty mins.

Flash Flood

Driving out of the parking lot, Misty jumps on Lake Shore Drive and heads out to Skokie. She parks the rental in the driveway and takes out her iPad to disable his security cameras.

After she put her iPad away, she hops out the car and rings the doorbell. As she walks in, she is greeted by the strong aroma of burning incense.

"Hey, stranger!" he greets. Misty walks right past him and heads to the bathroom in the master bedroom. Silently, Misty starts taking off her clothes and jumps in the shower. She put on the blue laced thong panties he had laid on the bathroom counter and slipped on the matching 6" blue laced heels. She returns to the bedroom, grabs a pillow, lays on her stomach, and slightly parts her legs.

"Damn!" he exclaimed. "Let's get straight to it, then."

He gets on the bed and seductively puts a blue blindfold on her. He caresses the middle of her back. "Get on your knees," he orders. Misty positions herself in doggy style and arched her back exposing the lace of her thong for his view. He begins to rub his hands all over her ass and massages her cheeks. Misty spreads her legs a little wider and jiggles her ass for his pleasure.

He spanks both sides and begins kissing her cheeks.

He pulls her panties to the side and gently blows cool air up and down her opening. He licks the crack of her ass then sticks his stiff tongue deep in her hole. Misty's bites her bottom lip to prevent her moaning sounds he loves to hear. He begins to tongue fuck her ass. Every stroke of his tongue released warm juices. Shoving his face between her legs, he starts sucking her pussy through her panties that were now soaked in her cum. Misty kept smearing her juices on his goatee, grinding her pussy and riding his face to orgasm. Her head falls back as she squirts flooding his face as she promised.

Feeling loose, she gets up and drops her cum-soaked panties on the floor. She grabs her clothes, heads to the bathroom, and looks down at her watch. *Fuuuck it's 4:45 a.m.* She quickly washes up, gets dressed, and walks out the door without saying a word.

Business is Business

At 9:03 a.m., Misty logs into her video conference. She was happy to see that her entire executive leadership team was all there waiting on her.

"Good morning, everyone! This meeting is going to be very short and sweet, especially since I have my Ethiopian coffee beans brewing as we speak. Thanks for hooking me up, Genet. Ok, listen up. I want to touch base and go over the next steps as it relates to securing the contract with Webb Protect. I will be meeting with Marcus today at 11 a.m. to finalize the contract. The plan is to have the contract signed and the advancement check in my hand when I leave today. Things are going to be moving rather quickly, so I hope everyone is caught up with their portfolios for our current clients. New business does not mean we neglect old business. Please send me your updates and any portfolios that need to be approved by the end of business today. Does anyone have any questions?"

"Yes, Misty, the bags have arrived. Have you decided on the list of items to put in them?" asks Nita, Misty's administrative assistant.

Nita was fairly new to the TechNiche team. She came highly recommend by Mallory, Misty's personal banker. She was a quiet girl, and Misty quickly noticed that Nita was eager to learn the business. It was so noticeable, Misty asked Nita if she wanted to run her own business one day. She was sharp, so Misty could definitely see it happening.

"Nita, I'll send you a list of those items this afternoon. Anyone else?"

"I got a question too. So will this advancement include raises?" asks Misty's Chief Financial Officer Britney, as she grabs a handful of Cheerios and throws them in her mouth.

"Yes, Brit, for you, it will be a gallon of milk to go with that dry ass cereal you keep munching in our ears during this call."

The team shares a laugh.

"On a serious note, I want to thank each and every one of you for stepping up this past year. Your hard work and support is not overlooked.

Everyone will be recognized as we continue to grow TechNiche. The goal this year is what?"

"Three offices, two cities, one TechNiche," they all said in unison.

The coffee pot alarm goes off, signaling to Misty that her brew was ready. She ends the call to prepare for the meeting with Webb Protect. Misty unties her silk scarf and begins to untwist her natural hair to create her professional look for the meeting. She dresses in her black blazer with wide-leg pants and navy blue buttoned shirt. Her favorite shoes from the Aminah Abdul Jillil's collection, the black peep-toe bootie pumps, made an excellent addition to her wardrobe. Not to mention the fact that they displayed her freshly manicured toes. Humming to herself in the mirror, she puts in three-carat diamond stud earrings and latches a Talley and Twine watch around her wrist. She applies a brown liquid lipstick by L'Oréal to her full lips, then sprays a little perfume behind her ears and on her wrists to complete the look. After one last twirl in front of the full-length mirror, she grabs her custom Zaaf laptop bag as she heads out the hotel suite.

At 12:40 p.m., Misty walks through the revolving door to the building's security desk. She shows the guard her identification card and is handed a visitor's badge. Once she scans her badge to the elevator, the door opens and an automated voice sounds across the speaker.

"Going up," said the male voice with a British accent, displaying the company name Webb Protect as well as the suite number. Misty exits the elevator and rings the doorbell. The receptionist buzzes her into the front office.

The receptionist, Ms. Sandra, is an elegant and fashionable older woman. Her glasses and fashion jewelry always match her outfits. Her wigs are ever-changing, and she still struts in her mini heels as if she were in her younger years. If you didn't know Ms. Sandra's personality, she comes across as a mean ole lady.

Misty and Ms. Sandra had a rocky beginning, but Misty learned quickly that Ms. Sandra is not a force to be reckoned with when it comes to business at the front desk of Webb Protect. Marcus was late at their first meeting, and Misty did not receive any email or phone call to notify her of his tardiness. Almost 15 minutes after their scheduled meeting time, Misty approached Ms. Sandra and asked if she had heard from him.

"He pays me to keep up with his schedule. He don't pay me enough to keep up with him," she spat, never looking up from her computer screen.

Misty gave her a look and went back to her chair. She sat thinking of ways to get more information from Ms. Sandra. Everyone knows secretaries always have more information than they share. Misty looked around and saw she had a few inspirational quotes on her desk. She took out a workbook from her Zaaf laptop bag and walked back to the desk.

"Ms. Sandra, I see you have a lot of inspirational words around your desk. I hope you enjoy this workbook," she said, placing the book on her desk. "I know the author personally. I think it will add to your inspiration."

Ms. Sandra picks up the workbook and reads the cover. "*Pardon me, I'm under construction. A woman's guide to rebuilding herself after losing everything.*" With her glasses hanging on her nose, she flips through the pages. "Seems interesting. It'll give me something to do while I'm up here. Thank you." With that, she places the workbook on her desk. After a few minutes of girl talk and chit-chatting, Ms. Sandra picks up the phone and immediately calls Marcus in a tone that summoned him to the front desk. Marcus has not been late to a meeting with Misty since that day.

Ms. Sandra walks around her desk and greets Misty with a big warm mama hug.

"Good morning, Ms. Sandra!"

"It's so good to see you, Suga. How was the flight coming in?"

"It wasn't too bad, I got in safely. I brought you the gospel CD I promised," said Misty as she handed her the case.

"You didn't forget about me. Thanks, Suga. I don't care what nobody say, my CD player ain't going nowhere. I've been writing in that workbook you gave me. Honey, them yielding signs be saving me from me," Ms. Sandra jokes as she escorts Misty to the conference room.

"I have the room set up for you and Marcus. Help yourself to coffee, water, and a few snacks. If you need me, just dial zero, Baby." Sandra walks out and closes the door behind her.

Misty walks into the large conference room that has four huge windows overlooking Lake Shore Drive and Lake Michigan. In the center of the room was a wooden table that seats 20 people, with two telephone docks in the center.

On one side of the wall sits a 65-inch television with cameras for video conferencing. The other wall has a Webb Protect logo in orange.

Misty reaches for her laptop and places it on the table. After checking her email and delegating a few tasks to her personal assistant, she heard a beep as Marcus appeared on the screen. He has on a white long sleeve shirt with white sapphire cufflinks and a grey vest with a matching tie.

"Good morning, Misty," says Marcus.

"Good morning, Marcus," Misty smiles.

"Please make yourself comfortable. I'll be in there shortly." Marcus winks at Misty before the screen turns off.

Misty grabs a bottle of water from the snack table and walks over to the windows. She admires the view of all the cars stuck in traffic on Chicago's Lake Shore Drive and looks out at the calm waves of Lake Michigan glistening from the sunshine. Marcus enters the conference room and places his portfolio on the table next to the seat of Misty's laptop. He grabs a bottle of water, walks over to the window, and stands next to Misty.

"Why should I hire your firm, Misty?" asks Marcus.

Misty turns to look at him. "Marcus, we've been through this before, and I'll remind you every time you think about not working with us. We are the best diverse women in tech. We have the best developers, engineers, and data scientists, with the top of the line strategists in finance for security. Quite frankly, your portfolio looks pitiful without TechNiche in it."

Marcus smiles and sips on the bottle of water. "Your prices are the highest amongst your competitors," he said seriously.

"Marcus, I don't compete. I lead. That's the price for the best. I have a 3-year contract for those companies that feel the need to build trust and a 7-year contract for those companies who have the balls to build with us."

Marcus chuckles and takes another sip of water. He walks to the conference table and pulls out her chair. "Sounds fair, which contract did you bring for me?"

Misty walks over, sits in the chair, and replies, "I brought my balls just in case you didn't have any."

Marcus laughs.

Dinner with Lathan

Misty accepted Lathan's invitation to dinner. It was one of his many attempts to try to repair what was left of their friendship. Misty gets dressed in her blue Russo romper by designer Andrea Iyamah. The romper was her favorite piece from the collection, because it shows her thick thighs and long legs. She slips on her black cross strap wedges and grabs her matching clutch. With one last makeup check in the mirror by the door, she heads out to Geja's Cafe.

Misty walks into the dimly lit restaurant and immediately spots Lathan seated in a cozy corner.

The hostess walks her over and offers Misty a seat as she lit the fondue flame. "Your waiter will be right with you," she adds before leaving Misty and Lathan alone at the table.

"I ordered you a glass of wine, Babe. Appetizers are on the way. I told the waiter to give us some random dipping sauces for us to try." He hands Misty a stick and begins to roast a marshmallow.

"Still hiding me in the cut, huh? How did you find out about this place?" Misty asks.

"We're not hiding, and a friend recommended it to me."

"The baby mama friend or the girlfriend? I have to be specific when asking about your friends," Misty sarcastically responds and sips on her glass of wine.

"Are we going to enjoy each other's company, or are we getting in the boxing ring for the fight you've been wanting to have? I didn't come here for this shit today, Misty."

Before Misty could respond, the waiter brought appetizers and carefully placed the dishes in the center of the table. It was a full spread with beef tenderloin, Australian lobster tail, gulf shrimp, fresh sea scallops, boneless chicken breast, assorted bell peppers, broccoli, mushrooms, potatoes, and onions.

"Wow, you went all out. It looks like our last supper. You sure I'm not taking food out of your baby's mouth?" Misty asks.

Lathan leans over. "It's been twenty fucking years Misty!" he hissed. "Twenty fucking years of this same bullshit ass argument! I had a baby while we were fucking! Goddamn, can we get past this shit and move the fuck on? Can we talk about something else?"

"Hmmm, I don't think I've ever heard you say it out loud Lathan. Had I known I was just a fuck, I would have never agreed to move in with you." Misty grabs a shrimp and dips it in a sauce. Lathan takes it out of her hand and eats it.

"Still taking shit from me. My respect, dignity, and pride wasn't enough? You know how it feels for me to find out you're having a baby the same fucking day I'm laid up in another hospital going through a fucking miscarriage by myself? If you do, please share that information with me cause I've been numb for the last twenty fucking years. You broke me, Lathan." Misty tries to hold in her tears and sips on the glass of wine. "I gave you everything and lost me in the process. Fuck you and the damn horse you rode in on, Lathan! Fuck you!"

Misty attempts to get up from the table, but Lathan grabbed her hand.

"What do you want from me, Misty?" Lathan pleads. "I don't know what else to do! I have been apologizing for years! I've been begging you to forgive me! I don't know what else to do!"

"Lathan, you've apologized," she said as she sits back down, "but you've never said I'm sorry." Her cell phone vibrates, and she removes her phone from her clutch.

My tongue is free tonight.

I'll be there in an hour.

Misty puts her cellphone on the table. She looks up, and Lathan is staring at her.

"You know what I miss? Your hugs. I miss your laugh. I miss going places with you and you having me trying all those crazy-ass foods. I miss your energy. I miss *you*, Babe. I don't even know why you hit me up, but I'm glad you did," Lathan confessed.

"Hell, I don't know either. You caught me on an off day. I've been back and forth through this city for a year trying to lock in this deal. Every time I thought to hit you up, I'd say 'fuck it.' I needed your hug too," said Misty.

Lathan's phone begins to vibrate and a photo pops up on the screen. *Is that...?*

Chapter 6
Blue – Hoe-ly Spirit

When it comes to sex, whether through personal experience, shared stories, or pure curiosity, I have read all about it and tried most of it. Now, I talk freely about it. I don't know about you, but one of my goals in this life we live is to be fucked in as many positions I come across. I plan to freely discover all the ways my body can orgasm. One way I am currently doing that is by fulfilling every fantasy I could ever imagine. I am not afraid to be the huntress and take what I want from a man, but I also crave to be ravished and dominated.

The hardest part of the night was having to wash off Eric's scent when he left. Bitch! My legs were sore as fuck, but my body was relaxed. I mustered up as much energy as I could and walked in the bathroom as my organs slowly shifted back in their normal placement. Eric fucked me up, but Bitch I handled that dick. He can definitely get it again. I stood in the mirror and fuck what you heard about a glow. Biiiitch, the radiance I had on my face was fucking *amazing*! Yaaasss, Bitch! He deserved a high five. Tonight was absolutely amazing.

I thought to myself, *Blue, Bitch, you did that!* The remnants of this man on my tongue, Honey. Ahem, I don't know what's got my throat itching. Hell, it's probably some of them kids I swallowed in there fighting! I don't know.

Chile, listen. One sec. Lemme clear my throat and cough up this man's cum that is trying to restrict my airflow. Cause a bitch ain't bout to die from sucking dick. Blue's cause of death is not going to be she didn't swallow all the kids. Bitch, no. That will *not* be on my death certificate as the reason Blue dies, Bitch. No.

Quick Hoe-lesson: Let me hip y'all hoes to something real quick. After you suck the dick, DO NOT, I REPEAT DO NOT brush your teeth! You do not want to expose your gums to sexually transmitted diseases and infections in your mouth. You gotta wash out your mouth and gargle with salt and warm water to cleanse your palate. You have to wait a few hours to brush your teeth. You're welcome.

Anyway, let me pour another glass of Meiomi wine, so we can sip and have some girl time. I want to talk about the hoe move y'all just witnessed. I told y'all I'm going to discover all the ways I can orgasm. The deep stroking, hair pulling, ass slapping, gut banging, waist gripping, neck choking, toe-curling, leg shaking, shit-talking, sweet pain kinda sex. I mean... I want it all!

Y'all ever look at somebody and wonder why he/she is always mean, rude, or moody? I chalk it up to them not getting fucked right. For real. I tell those types of people to tap into their hoe-ly spirit. Life is too short to be that miserable, and all you gotta do is get some pussy or dick to at least make you feel better.

Y'all know what hoeism is? Yes? No? Well, here's how I define it. Hoeism is the belief that fucking, having sex, getting your back blown out, umm.....engaging in sexual intercourse for those technical people, releases your mind from the stress levels, distractions, and blockages a person experiences in life. That's my definition. I promise you, tapping into your hoeism allows you to think clearly. Try it, and you'll find yourself in a better mood.

Society has put this negative spin on hoes. Everyone has a lil' hoe in them, most are just embarrassed to say it exists within them because of the stigma that comes with it. Listen, you don't have to sleep with more than one person to practice hoe shit. You can have one person you do a whole bunch of hoe shit with. And I don't judge. If you choose to do hoe shit with a lot of people, wrap it up, practice safe sex, and keep it moving.

We all have a little hoe in us. Every time I see Reign or Misty getting bitchy or fussing over petty shit, that's where I come in. I tap into that hoeism. You gotta tap into the power within Honey. The hoe-ly spirit is there to lead you along the way. Each and every one of us has our own individual needs. It all depends on the mood. At times, you just want to have sex, so you can sneak in a quickie to knock the edge off and go about your business. Boom! Then, at times, you want to make love, get the soft touch, be held, and be dubbed queen of foreplay. Then there are times, Bitch, you want to be bent over, spanked, and fucked till your pussy is sore. That's my ass. Fuck me 'til I apologize for showing up with panties, okay? Sip.

With Misty, I can kinda get away with a few things because she understands that sometimes you gotta bust a nut and keep it moving. It's either to start off her day right or release the stress of the day. Again, it all depends on the mood. On the other hand, Reign ass, she be on some bullshit sometimes. She be on that sneaky shit too. She be having these damn church people talking her into bullshit ass stuff with no damn co-signer.

Honey, one day Reign had these fools convince her that celibacy was a good idea.

Yeah...nah. I mean, managing your sexual appetite is an acquired behavior, but we not about to be doing this. I was not trying to participate in this group activity she was trying to have with us. I'm not suffering because these horny ass heffas' husbands at the church not fucking them right. Girl, if you don't run me my dick! She was about to make me lose my whole religion, and I'm barely holding on to the one I got. Don't the bible say He came to save us all? Bitch, we can repent in the morning because I plan on fucking tonight Sis.

There was this one other time these same women at the church put Reign in charge of the midweek lesson. I'm not going to judge, but I'mma talk about they raggedy asses, though. Reign asked them to pick a woman in the Bible they could relate to and come to the class to share with everyone why they picked her. I merely suggested that she should study Delilah. Reign got an attitude. I don't know why, though. See, Delilah, she's my girl. I love her story. She was a seductive and wily temptress. She was so good at luring, enticing, and tempting men; she got them to do what she wanted them to do. Of course, Reign rejected my suggestion. That's not the side of her she brings to the church house, although she could relate very well with Delilah. I got her ass though, hehehe. It happened in Jamaica for Storm's wedding, and his name was Lorenz Knight.

Chapter 7
Reign - Knight of Pleasure

Reign lounges by the poolside, taking advantage of the quiet time before the butler wakes everyone up for breakfast. She listens to the crashing waves and admires the breathtaking view of the sunrise in Jamaica. Footsteps quietly approach the pool area.

"Excuse me," says Storm, "Ain't you supposed to be doing something around here? Blowing up a balloon, picking up flowers, ironing out tablecloths... something? I mean, what are you doing? My maid of honor does not have the luxury of laying around a pool—or anywhere for that matter—hours before my wedding. This is simply unacceptable."

Reign lifts her Chanel sunglasses giving Storm the deadliest look. "Bitch. I am in

Jamaica, relaxing by the poolside after experiencing a majestic view of the sunrise. Here yo black ass go blocking my sunshine with all this negative energy! Why won't you just let me be great?"

Storm laughs, throws her towel on the chair, and fixes her large sun hat before sitting next to Reign. "I was looking out the window and told Anderson I was coming out here to fuck with you." She puts on her Hollywood designed Prada sunglasses and stretches her legs out on the pool chair.

"Between you and Anderson," Reign shrugs. "Y'all both get on my damn nerves. Fuck you and him. He already on my shit list with this fucking red dress he got me wearing."

"That's y'all thing. I'm not getting in the middle of it. I say something, then turn around and get cussed out by both y'all crazy asses. Leave me out of it."

"Reign, we were walking around the resort last night and this is the amazing view we woke up to this morning. Bitch, the website didn't do this place justice. This villa is gorgeous! It's just the right size for everybody to be comfortable in one place. We got a maid, a cook, and a butler. I can't wait to see the dolphins later. Yeah, we gotta come back again."

"I told you that you'd love it here," says Reign. "I can't wait 'til you hear the band later. Bitch, you ready to say I do? You better be. Yo ass getting married tuhday even if I have to drag yo muthafucking ass down the damn aisle myself."

"I don't have a choice now, I guess. I've been procrastinating long enough. We're all here—

his family, my family, our kids, and all our friends. People paid lots of money. I told Anderson that he better not mess up. I'll snatch up one of these fine ass Jamaicans and drop y'all asses off at the airport."

The butler announces that breakfast was ready. Reign and Storm get up to walk over to the table to join the family coming out of their rooms in the villa.

"Is that a goddamn blunt?" Reign exclaims. "Where Anderson find weed at? Dang, we ain't been here 24 hours!"

"Girl, you're late," laughs Storm. "He asked the people at the front desk where he could get some of the good weed, and they sold it to him right on the spot. You can't come to Jamaica and not get the weed. That's illegal."

"I swear, can't take black folk nowhere!" Reign sighs as she takes a seat.

The table was set up outside by the pool. It was covered in a white tablecloth, with petals of the native pink and red hibiscus flowers beautifully scattered across the center. There were two tall pitchers placed on opposite ends of the table. One was filled with Jamaica's famous and refreshing sorrel punch with orange slices, and the other was filled with the famous rum punch. The seasoned chef cleverly blended the traditional Jamaican and American breakfast styles to accommodate everyone.

While everyone was chatting at the table, Reign noticed two men walking through the villa toward them. It was Ant, the DJ she hired for the wedding, and an unknown male. While the men greeted everyone with their hellos at the table, Reign could feel the unknown male looking at her. She makes eye contact with him, and a heatwave passes through her as she blushes.

Reign gets up and asks Ant to walk back inside. She wanted to give him his deposit and the playlist for the wedding reception. Storm followed behind her and walked over to the unknown man. By the time they left, Storm gave Reign all the details.

"His name is Lorenz Knight, he is 39, and has a 5-year-old son. He has never been married and doesn't have a girlfriend. His mother passed a few years ago, which is a blessing. Well, not a blessing like that. You know what I mean. Bitch, you won't have any mother-in-law issues. He owns a plumbing business in Chicago, Bitch, so you know he can lay some pipes! Haha! He is in Jamaica visiting Anthony for a few days. They went to school together."

Storm took a sip of her rum punch to catch her breath. "Oh, yeah, and I think you should fuck him," she adds matter of factly.

"Oh, my God. I can't stand yo ass. Bitch, you just met the man five minutes ago!" Reign exclaimed.

"Shhhhhiiiid, that's all the time I need to get the 4-1-1. Bitch! I didn't say *marry* him, just, you know, wet his beard while you here."

"Soooo inappropriate! I can't stand you!" Reign laughs. Her mouth waters at the thought.

***

Hello, fitted and healthy beard, I thought as I climb into the boat docked on the shore of the Caribbean Sea. The full moon shines bright as its reflection straddles the sea. Lust crashes my flesh. Our eyes lock. Daring. Alone. The moment we've been flirting with since we met. I'm sitting across from you on your blanket. I'm ready to teach you the art of satisfaction on how to touch me in a way my body will produce juices you didn't even know you craved. How do you want me? On your face? Your dick in my mouth? On my side? On my back? Bent over? You pull my sundress over my head. You notice my nipples respond to the light breeze from the sea. I watch you take my breast in your mouth and bite my nipple tenderly. When I lay on my back and you pull me by the legs, a surge of warmth takes over me. You lift my legs and run your hands along the side of my thighs. You touch me and notice I'm wet. Your tongue on my clit captures my drip. I don't know if it was the feel of your hands or how much I enjoy watching you have your way with me. You stand in the boat and put my hand on the bulge of your dick. I take off your pants and pull it out. As I marvel at the beauty of God's handiwork, I tell you to sit down because I want your dick in my mouth. I love your taste and the feel of your dick rubbing against my throat. I eased myself up and guided you inside of me, craving the stroke of your dick even more. I slowly move my hips back and forth to adjust to your width. You grip the flesh in my ass as I ride your dick. With all the kissing, licking, touching, tasting, feeling, fingering, biting, fucking, spanking, caressing, pinching, and nibbling, I lost my mind in pleasure. I shudder. I could no longer hold back. I release what you were looking for and craved, the sound of me moaning your name...'

***

"Reign....Reign....Reign!   Helloooooo, Reign?" Storm snaps her fingers.

"Huh?"

"Bitch, I didn't say fuck him right now wit yo horny ass. The makeup artists just walked in, and they waiting on us."

"My bad," Reign laughs, "Let's go get you married."

Chapter 8
Misty - Take it to the Bank

Misty sat in her Atlanta office and stared at the check. *Pay to the Order of TechNiche, Inc.* She looked out the window and whispered, "Thank you!"

She knew TechNiche was going to finally get the recognition both the company itself and the women who worked in it deserved. After logging the check from Webb Protect into the system, she did a few other administrative duties—responded to a few emails, listened to routed voicemails, and noted who she needed to call back. She locked her laptop and walked the check over to Britney's office.

"Brit, here's the green light we were waiting for. I approved the budget. Please start making the travel arrangements for the team meeting in Belize and process the checks for their bonuses," Misty instructed.

"Weeeeee, we're going to Belize! Ooo, I can't wait!" Britney spins around in her office chair.

"Shhhh, quit being so damn loud. Remember that this is a *business* trip."

"You walked in here like this wasn't a big deal. I knew you would get the account. We about to be put on the map! Go look in the closet."

"What did you buy?" Misty asks.

"Would you go look?" Britney says sternly.

Misty walked to the closet and pulled out an oversized tote bag with the company logo on a picture of a globe. "This is too cute!" she gushes.

"Well, everybody's gonna need a carry-on, so why not one with the TechNiche logo?" states Britney.

Misty ran back over to Britney's desk and gave her a hug. They both embraced and shed a few tears. Britney has been by Misty's side since the first business class they shared in college. Misty would talk for hours to Britney about TechNiche. Britney would listen and tease her about making sure TechNiche paid CFOs six figures to keep her figure right. As they grew, Misty kept her team small intentionally because she always planned to one day take her team to Belize. Now ten years later, she would be able to live the dream she spent so many hours daydreaming about.

There was a knock on the door, and the two ladies jumped with surprise.

"Wipe your face," Britney whispers as Nita walks into the office.

"Mallory called and wanted to meet with you today. She said it was urgent."

"Thanks, Nita, please clear my schedule for the rest of the evening," Misty replies. With a nod, Nita walks out.

"Can you handle things while I run to the bank?" Misty asks.

"Gotcha girl. Congratulations! Lemme make this deposit real quick and book this trip!"

***

Misty walks in and is welcomed by a short man dressed in a black three-piece suit standing at the check-in counter of the bank. He had black hair which was graying around the edges.

"Welcome to Best Bank. How may I help you?" he greets.

"Hi, I'm Misty. I'm here to see Mallory."

"Right this way, ma'am. She's expecting you."

The greeter escorts Misty to Mallory's office. Misty looks through the glass on the side of the office door and sees Mallory on the phone. She waves to indicate that it was okay to enter and quickly ends her call. The guard opens the door, and Mallory asks him to leave the two ladies alone in the room. Mallory offers Misty a seat.

"I'm glad you were able to come in as quickly as you did. How are you, Misty?"

"You said it was urgent, and you didn't leave any details with Nita."

"Misty, I asked you to come in because we won't be able to cash the check from Webb Protect. The bank froze your business account."

"Excuse me? The bank did what?" Misty gasped.

"We had to freeze your business account. You're currently being investigated for money laundering."

"WHAT! You're joking, right? There has got to be some kind of mistake somewhere because I didn't launder any fucking thing anywhere! Mal, you know me! I've been doing business here for years!" Misty exclaimed.

"Shhhhh! Misty, I can lose my job for even calling you in here to give you a heads up. I have 48 hours to submit your account statements to FinCEN," Mallory explained.

"I can't lose my business. I got a lot of people depending on me!" Misty cries out.

"You need to get a lawyer, and you need to get one fast!" Mallory replied and handed Misty a folder.

Misty walked out of the bank in disbelief. She did not know who to call or what to do. She sat in her car with disbelief, sadness, and anger. *What the fuck is going on?* she wondered as the tears starting to flood from her face.

Chapter 9
Blue – At the darkest hue

I really needed a moment to have an ugly face cry. I needed to laugh. To be celebrated. To save myself. To be selfish. To stop and be held. To think of no one but myself. Many times we all need a moment to just...be.

I hate the days I'm triggered into giving a fuck. It's so draining. Truthfully, I talk a lot of shit, but damn! I'm human too. No one ever questioned what made me this way. I'm just fucking branded as a whore and a home-wrecking bitch. Tonight, I lay alone in the center of my queen size bed wrapped up in my baby blue 1200 thread count Pima cotton comforter. All I had were feelings of solitude, loneliness, isolation, and frustration. I was drained, tired, embarrassed, used, and certainly disappointed. Where is this strong woman everyone sees? It just isn't a good day for me.

People say, "If walls could talk, the things they would say!" Here I lay staring and wondering what my ceiling had witnessed over the past few years. The reality is that the walls are so common that the ceiling is often overlooked. It has watched me stay up at night, crying out wondering why a man did not want me or would not love me. It has watched me compromise myself and settle for less than I deserve, only to receive even less than that. I know it has seen these feather-filled pillows collect many of my tears during my lonely nights. Each time I was frustrated, drained, tired, embarrassed, used, and certainly disappointed. Yes, my ceiling has seen me broken. To protect myself, I mastered how to have emotionless sex.

This ceiling has viewed the backs of different men and overheard the whispers of how good my pussy has been to them. For a long time, I had three positions: face riding, reverse cowgirl, and doggy style. Each night, I searched for the same outcome and didn't need to see his face to achieve my goal—bust a few nuts between 11:00 p.m. and 2:00 a.m. This ceiling has also observed these same men barely washing off the scent of our sex from their dicks, only to get up and leave to go home.

Now I'm dealing with a different kind of demon. This bastard has a disrespectful way of showing up in my fucking life at my darkest fucking moments, UNINVITED! It takes over my thoughts even when I try to ignore it. It takes over my body, and I make rash decisions with unknown men to knock the edge off when I'm horny. Sometimes at my lowest points, I could have someone in my bed, and it will sneak in and lay right next to me. His spirit is called Loneliness. Loneliness will make you do some things that make you question your own character.

I am alone, and my companions are my own thoughts. If I'm not careful, Loneliness has a way of convincing me to take residence in its house called Isolation. I walk into Isolation and find myself calling me names that I know do not define me: stupid, crazy, idiot, and a dumb ass fool!

Loneliness took mental notes of the times I felt guilt, shame, or embarrassment and tied it to a memory frame. He hung those frames on the wall of Isolation as decorations. My feelings of my sins have hung on the walls for years.

They serve as a mosaic reminder of the many unwise decisions I made when loneliness visited me. Isolation felt familiar. Actually, this place is now beginning to feel like home.

Chapter 10
Reign – With clouds of controversy

"It is such an honor to be invited to GraceStone. The hospitality of the women's ministry has been nothing short of amazing. Look at all the ladies looking so beautiful in their good ole traditional red and black church colors."

The congregation laughs in agreement.

Reign stood conflicted. She couldn't decide if she was going to use this moment to exploit her personal life. Still, by the sudden surge within her body, she felt goosebumps as her heart took over her mind. She was no longer afraid.

"Today, I ask everyone this morning to do the very thing the title of my workbook says.

Pardon me, I'm under construction. I finally understand what it means to be hidden behind Calvary's cross. I agree. Hide me because after today, I might be stoned to death once His people see my sins on this pulpit that THEY made."

The congregation quieted down.

"Thanks, Pastor Shepherd, for allowing me to be here. I didn't take this invitation lightly. I know I have a responsibility. A lot of times, when I'm invited to speak, I question God. I mean, what is He thinking? He must have dialed the wrong number. But today, I know He called the right one cause I got time today." Reign picks up her iPad, takes off her heels, and takes a seat comfortably at the center of the stage.

"A few years ago," she says, as she crosses her legs at her ankles, "A friend of mine gave me a CD. Yeah, a CD. I know I'm dating myself. It was entitled *10 things every single person should do,* by Bishop TD Jakes. He said a lot of things, but what stood out for me that I totally agreed with was when he said, 'If someone got in the pulpit and really prayed, it would clean this church out; because people couldn't handle prayer, real prayer UNLEASHED'!" Reign goes through her iPad and taps a few times then places it next to her.

"I want to thank my family and friends for coming out to support me, especially my fiancé Brandon and his wife, Christine."

The congregation gasps!

"Recently, I found out that I was in a relationship with Brandon, who would turn around and marry Christine while we were together. I met Brandon a couple of years ago, and after a year of him chasing me, I finally gave him a chance. I should have done my research as his wife suggested. See, she called me New Year's Day at 3 o'clock in the morning to let me know I was sleeping with her husband. Her words were more explicit, but I'll try to keep it PG for the kids. If I did my research, Brandon wouldn't have gotten to my heart through his lies. But you know, I was vulnerable and weak. He was so good that my common sense went out the door."

The entire congregation was in a panic, and some people began to get up to leave while others sat and mumbled in disbelief. The extra nosey people began making shushing sounds to try to quiet down the noise level so they could hear the rest of what Reign had to say.

"I had gotten used to his silent rejection. The days of him walking around the house mad, not saying a word to me, became normal. One morning—I guess it may have been his wedding day—he was restless the whole night before. When he got up, I told him that I would no longer put up with his behavior. He stormed out the house.

"You see, I tried to hold him to a level of expectations and standards that I needed from him as a man, and he stripped me down and reduced me to a whining bitch. Yet he became everything I needed him to be for me and gave of himself so freely to another woman. He returned from 'work', unbeknownst to me, with a whole wife, two kids, and a dog." Reign watched as the people in the sound ministry tried to figure out how to turn off her mic.

"The night I found out he was married, I was devastated, heartbroken, pissed, and, most of all, I was embarrassed. I thought I had my forever when, in reality, I was only his pastime when he needed to relieve himself or was bored. Why did he come into my life to use me? Cheat on me? Treat me like crap? And then, go get married to someone else? Do you know what that does to a person?

"For a long time, I questioned myself. He was able to convince me that he was the prize in our entire relationship. I lost myself in the process of finding ways to love him. I found myself accepting his inappropriate behavior because I wanted to be with the person he said he was when I first met him. The way he treated me caused me to look at myself and question who I was as a person. What was it about me he didn't like? Was it my hair? My weight? My strong personality? Maybe it was my bad attitude. How could I miss it?

"For a year, I stayed, hoping and praying that one day he would morph into the potential I had spent so much time daydreaming he would eventually become for me. When it was just the two of us, I would sometimes see the loving, kind, gentle, vulnerable man I desired him to be. Never once did I consider that it was my illusion of him that I created.

"I tried to be the best woman for him, and it wasn't good enough. You know why? Because he wasn't *mine!* I gave him my life based on the empty promises and words of, 'One day Babe,' 'Just wait, Babe,' 'Your time will come,' 'Eventually,' 'Soon,' and 'We'll get there.' I made room for him in my heart and my life with my family and friends. I freely welcomed him in my home while he filled me up with promises of so many tomorrows that never came.

"I gave that man everything, no matter the cost. The highest price I paid was at the expense of *me!* It became expensive holding on to a man that wasn't mine to begin with. It cost me everything—my self-esteem, my self-respect, my dignity, my pride, my joy, my friends, and my family! I lost myself! Then one day, I stood in the mirror and could no longer recognize the reflection I saw in front of me."

It wasn't until Reign felt something wet on her chest that she realized she was crying. She could no longer hold back the tears that escaped. Reign wipes her face and picks up the iPad and images rotated on the large screens in the sanctuary.

"Today, I sit here with the blackmail text messages from Brandon and Christine threatening to release the nude photos I shared with my *fiancé*. I also have copies of my bank statements showing ATM withdrawals and transfer of funds. They were draining my personal bank account and sending money to their own accounts. I got credit card bills paying their bills. I even have my foreclosure letter since I trusted him to the mortgage on the house.

"I don't know how and I don't know when, but I'm going to get back everything Brandon and Christine took from me, and I'm charging double with interest."

Chapter 11
Mist-ery Business

"Lemme get a blowjob, Darius!" Misty yells at the bartender. She throws her purse on the counter and jumps on the seat of the swing at the bar.

Darius turns around and looks at her. "Must have been a rough day," he mutters as he places a wine glass in the overhead rack. Darius has a slight accent that followed his words when he spoke. If you listened to him long enough, it felt as though he was caressing you without even touching you.

"Darius, just make me the damn drink," Misty replies and starts rummaging through her purse.

He chuckles and places an empty shot glass on the counter. "You want to talk about it?" he asks.

"Nope."

Misty's phone vibrates. She looks at the text.

You seem stressed.

Darius checks the overstocked bar, pulls the Kahlua and Bailey's from the shelf, and begins to make her drink. He quickly turns around to grab the whipped cream to top off her shot. Misty covers the glass with her mouth and knocks it back.

"No hands. Impressive. Must have been a really bad day," says Darius.

Misty slams the shot glass on the counter. "I fucked up!" she screamed as she drops her head on the counter.

"This sounds like you need a shot of vodka." Darius poured a shot of premium vodka in her glass. She took the shot and got up to leave. "Add it to my tab and make sure you tip yourself fifty. We'll talk about it next time." Misty straightened her clothes and walked out of the bar.

Misty sits in her Jeep and pulls out her phone and replies to the message.

Meet me in thirty.

Misty reached down and pulled her panties to the side. She pulled his dick out and sat on it, releasing a sigh of relief. Passionately, she massaged his tongue with her own while riding the hell out of his dick. "Why are you fucking me so good?" she moaned.

"You're on top, so you're the one fucking me," he replied raspily.

He lifted Misty from the couch and carried her into her room. Out the corner of his eye, he spotted her vibrator on the nightstand. He cuffed her to the bedpost and ran his against her body. He pulled down her panties and threw it on the floor. He put a pillow under her lower back and began stroking her with his dick while applying the vibrator to her clit. The buzzing sound, the stroke of his dick, and the sound of her moaning was too sensational to handle. She couldn't hold it in. Misty squirted, and he pulled out, so he could come down and eat her pussy. In turn, she sucked the soul out of him. As he was about to cum, she opened her mouth as wide as she could, taking in the length of his dick. As the warm stream shot into her throat, she swallowed every single bit of it.

Code Red: Keep your mouth shut

It had been twenty hours since Misty received the devastating news about her bank account at Best Bank. She knew she had to put her big girl panties on and make some tough decisions. The tears were not going to resolve the problem she had going on with the bank, so she got on the phone with Britney.

"Code Red," says Misty solemnly.

"I'm on my way."

When Misty walked into Panera Bread with the folder Mallory gave her, Britney was already seated with two cups of coffee and two cinnamon crunch bagels. Misty takes a seat at the table and sips her coffee.

"Bitch, the last time you used Code Red, I was picking yo ass up from Motel 6 after you bleached Lathan's clothes when you found out he had a baby on you," Britney joked as she sipped on her coffee. "That was over twenty years ago. The fuck is going on?"

"I went to the bank, Brit, and Mallory told me that TechNiche account is frozen. On top of that, she tells me that the Financial Crimes Enforcement has my account under investigation. We're talking Feds, Brit!"

"Is that what that bitch called you about the other day?" Britney asks. "How the fuck FinCEN get the account? What the fuck we paying Mallory ass for?"

"Brit, I'm so pissed," Misty sighed. "I left that fucking bank crying. I sat in my car shaking and just fucking crying."

"Nah, we pay that bitch too much fucking money for her to be slipping like this. FinCEN? Really? The fuck?" Britney grunts. She took the folder Misty had in her hand and looked at the account statements.

"I had to sit back and think cause you know me when my ass gets hit. I have 24 hours to grieve, then it's straight planning and plotting. I was really shook, then I looked at the account number."

"Something ain't right, Mist. This is the new account," says Britney as she continues to review the statements.

"Exactly! I looked over that statement and went through each page and every transaction. Then it hit me. First of all, why did Mallory call Nita and not my cellphone? And if she couldn't get me, why she ain't called you? Second, how she even know about the check from Webb Protect? I walked it over to you the day I logged it in. It wasn't even deposited yet." Britney sits back in the chair and places the folder on the table.

"She said she couldn't cash the check. What check? So I started to do some research. Bitch, look at this shit." Misty tosses Britney an envelope.

"WHAT THE FUCK? HOLY SHIT! NO FUCKING WAY!" Britney gasped. "Biiiitch! Where the fuck you get these pictures from?" Britney asks. She silently continues to flip through the four pictures in constant rotation.

"You know these Millennials post everything online. Social media is their life. This pic is Nita and her daddy Lathan. Here's one with Nita and her mother Christine. Look who's also standing at a baby dedication."

"Is that Mallory?"

"Girl yes! Here's one with Nita and Mallory. You see the caption at the bottom? God-mommy and me," Misty said sarcastically.

"But Nita's last name is Smith!"

"That was Christine's last name before she married Allen DeVaughn. I'm sorry, I mean

Brandon as he now introduces himself. Bitch, the code red baby is Nita."

"Bitch, the code red baby is NITA!" Britney repeats.

"If I keep thinking about how they tried to screw me, I'm going to burn some shit down. Mallory got FinCEN involved, so this is some next level shit, Bitch. I'm not doing federal time for a mere eleven million fucking dollars."

"How did you find out?" Britney asks.

"Nita called Lathan when we went out for dinner," says Misty.

"Wait, what? Dinner? When the fuck did this happen?" Britney asked in disbelief.

"The night before I left Chicago, I had dinner with Lathan. Don't ask me why I agreed, but I did. We started to argue, well, I started, but that's not the point. His phone began to vibrate. When I looked to see who it was, Nita's picture popped up under Baby Girl."

"One trip without me, and you done fucked a muthafucker named Eric, done had yo pussy ate by dude, and you having dinner with fucking Lathan only to find out Nita is his daughter. Bitch you doing too fucking much in a goddamn 48-hour trip! What the fuck is going on around here?!" Britney exclaims.

"I know." Misty lowers her head. "I sat up and cried for hours. Like why am I always being screwed by so many fucking people? It's been like this since as far as I can remember. I'm over it. Never again."

"This is not on you, Misty. Even people who betray you are a part of the plan. Don't say never again. Thank them for showing up. So, what's the plan? I know you got one."

"I sure the fuck do."

Baby Sings the Blues

The loud sirens blazed the Peachtree streets of Atlanta. The police cars surrounded TechNiche headquarters office. One officer had her in handcuffs, escorting her out of the building. He put the folder filled with documents in the front seat and opened the back door to push her head down to enter the back seat.

"Misty, can you please call my father? His name and number are on my emergency contact list," Nita asks from the back seat of the police car.

"I suggest you wait on that one phone call," says Misty. The officer closes the door. He walks around to the driver's side and drives off.

"Thanks for taking care of this for me. If you need anything else, let me know," Misty tells the chief of police handing him a folder.

"I'll text you. Make sure you bring those blue pumps I like," he responds.

"As long as you bring the cuffs," Misty winks and walks back into her office.

Mal-Practices – Misty Perfects

Misty sits at her desk and reads a Notice of Seizure from the IRS.

THESE PREMISES HAVE BEEN SEALED AND PROPERTY BLOCKED BY ORDER OF...

She hits the speed dial on her telephone.

"Hello", Mallory greets. Her voice shaking.

"You almost got me," Misty chuckles.

"You have until end of business to return the $500 thousand dollars I've paid you," Misty continued.

"Misty I don't have any money. You took everything from me," Mallory continues to hysterically cry.

"END OF BUSINESS!" Misty states firmly and ends the call.

She logs into the security cameras facing Mallory's house. She watches the men she hired repossess all of her personal property, cars, paintings, coin collections and jewelry.

Misty's cellphone rings.

"Hey Brit, what's up?" Misty greets.

"Everything taken care of on my end and Best Bank has termed her effective immediately," Britney replies.

"Good. There are packing her shit as we speak. The government can have whatever is left," Misty says.

"Ok, we'll catch up later," says Britney and ends the call.

A numb feeling of rage starts to take over Misty as she continues to look at her screen.

"I want every fucking thing," she whispers.

Chapter 12
Blue - When the skies are gray, I'll give you Blue.

"I sat with the anger long enough until she told me her name was Grief."

I swear I wish Misty would get over Lathan's ass. I know it's easier said than done. She's been wanting closure to move on for years. In life, you're going to go through some tough things and have to move on without an apology. Hell, you won't even get an "I'm sorry" or even any type of explanation. As women, we hold on to things for years, hoping to get answers on why a man would hurt us after we've been so good to him? Be confident in this—a man saying I'm sorry after hurting you will rarely ever happen!

When Misty miscarried, she changed. All you remember is a striking cramp and a shit load of blood. The procedure of laying on your back with feet in stirrups leaves you with so many unanswered questions. Was there only one baby that miscarried? What if I'm aborting a possible twin? What's this pinch? Am I supposed to feel numb? Even though Misty didn't have a baby, her body still went through changes. Breasts were leaking milk, and hips were sore from making room for a baby that was no longer there. In addition to the changes, no one gives you time to truly mourn the loss of the baby. It was a lot to process.

Misty finds out the one person she trusted, left her by herself to go through one of the most traumatic experiences a woman could go through in life. She suffered through this ordeal only to find out he was expecting a baby with another woman on the same day she miscarried. He gained what she lost. That's a low blow that takes every last breath out of a person. Head lowered, holding your chest, trying not to hyperventilate, slowly breathing in and out, waiting to exhale...it's a lot. All the while, you're just sinking. Sinking into a dark abyss without knowing if or when to come up for air. That shit is damaging. It would change anyone. That's a lot to take on at any age, much less at twenty years old.

For years, Misty struggled after all the noise was gone. You know....the noise of being in the headlines of the gossip news cycle of so-called friends and family. To avoid dealing with her hurt, she threw herself into her career and mastered the IT world. At home, she found herself alone with her thoughts and memories.

She recalled all she had done to make Lathan happy. It was a lot to take on all the while sacrificing herself. Misty gave the wrong person the responsibility to take care of her heart and ended up with a hole in the process.

Unfortunately, she can no longer be mad that her heart was returned broken. She has to cut her losses and know that she is responsible for her own heart. That continues to be her struggle, and the Bible tells you, "Above all else, guard your heart, for everything you do flows from it." Misty has to learn to share her heart, but she cannot put it in someone else's hands to take care of it.

Now the problem is learning to forgive in the absence of hearing or waiting for a person to say, 'I'm sorry.' You have to learn to forgive in order to move on. When you don't forgive, you leave your heart exposed to bitterness and insecurities. The Bible says, "The peace of God will keep your heart and mind." You have to put a guard over your heart.

I am a champion for therapy. I firmly believe that you have to carry the cross in order to wear the crown. Out of your heart flows the issues of life. You can't go around the issues or experiences you have in life—you have to go *through* them. There is nothing wrong with talking to someone to sort through your feelings.

This churchy polite superficial television censored Christian image that Reign projects, got her running around thirsting for someone to love her. Her heart gets carried away with every little compliment. Every nice person or anybody that smile; There she goes with all these ideas, fantasies, soul ties, and connecting to men emotionally with one-sided love affairs. That's how the fuck she ended up with Brandon punk ass.

I'm Blue. I'm a raging sea, trapped inside of a teardrop. I'm with the fuck shit and the muthafucking shenanigans! Misty and Reign put the lioness to sleep, and I woke up hungry for blood. In the land of the heartless, I was sure to give the ladies a warm welcome when they arrived.

Chapter 13
Reign – Better to Reign in Hell than serve in Heaven

Reign stood numb staring in a daze. Her vision became hazy and her mind filled with vile thoughts. She allowed her mind to have the self-imposed out of body experience she had denied herself for the past few months. Slowly, she tilted her head side to side, taking in the entire scene. It was both enticing and mesmerizing. She was in awe of how her mind visually separated each layer of color—black, red, orange, yellow, and white. She named each crackling and crumbling sound. The feeling still didn't satisfy the tears, sweat, sacrifices, hurt, and sleepless nights she was experiencing from the betrayal. She didn't realize how close she was.

Alas! finally! The heat from the burning building matched the rage she felt from within. The blazing noise of the sirens awakes Reign from her trance. *I wonder who called?* she thought as she turns around and walks toward her SUV.

Reign sat and watched as firefighters fought a losing battle against the raging flames engrossing the multi-million dollar mansion. As large sections of the roof caved in, the flames seemed endless. It continued to spread throughout the mansion until it reached every corner of the structure.

Reign peeked up at the side of her window to see four helicopters of the local news circle. The five-bedroom, five-bathroom mansion that covered 6,500 square-feet of Brookhaven. There was no amount of water in the fire engine tankers that could quench the thirst of revenge Brandon had left with Reign.

The phone rings, and it was Lathan. "Misty Blue Reign! Where the fuck is my daughter?"

The Reign of terror had just begun.

***

My Name is...let me explain.

I love my name. It is as unique as my fingerprint and identifying as my personality. So, let me formally introduce myself. This story has been about Me, Myself, and I. Together, you get all three of us: Misty Blue Reign.